The Story
of
Angel Fred

a Christmas fable
written by Ken Untener

A fictional Christmas story
(which draws considerably on the imagination,
and mixes two very different Gospel accounts)
dedicated to those
whose best-laid plans sometimes run **AMUCK**.

Illustration by Kay Wejrowski

Published by *Little Books* of the Diocese of Saginaw

ISBN: 978-0-9863344-2-9

Published by *Little Books* of the Diocese of Saginaw
P.O. Box 6009,
Saginaw, Michigan 48608-6653

www.littlebooks.org

Printed and bound
in the United States of America

The Beginning

It all started about 300 B.C.

Rumors had long buzzed among the angels about some big event called "Christmas." Word was out that it would happen soon, within a couple hundred years.

One day an angel named Fred was summoned to a closed door meeting in the front office. Fred was a great organizer. Although his compulsive planning usually drove everyone crazy, there was no arguing that he did good work. He even had a clean desk.

Fred came out of the meeting beaming. He had been put in charge of the logistics for the event called "Christmas."

The Planning Stage

Fred wasted no time getting to work.

The front office had given him some basic parameters (Fred loved that word): Publicity should be kept to a minimum; decorum was to be observed; and a few special features should be added here and there to give it a touch of class.

Within two weeks Fred had a rough draft with, indeed, some masterful touches. It would take place in a quiet hill town up north called Nazareth. A star in the sky would mark the occasion. An angelic choir would sing. Three Magi from the East would quietly bring gifts on behalf of the whole world.

There were a thousand other details, of course, but Fred prioritized them (another favorite word). He worked for 200 years and finally submitted a 700-page plan.

It came back stamped "Approved" and Fred was on cloud nine.

Final Preparations

With the big event only 100 years away, there was no time to waste.

Fred set up a central office with a sign on the door in big red and green letters: "Operation Christmas." He even made a scale model of Nazareth, exact to the smallest detail.

Day and night Fred worked on maps, charts, check lists... and memos.

Fred was big on memos.

The Countdown

The hundred years flew by. There was great excitement when Fred announced that Angel Gabriel's flight was only 30 days away. He posted the countdown in big red numbers outside his office (which he preferred to call the "Control Center").

He nearly drove Gabriel crazy, calling him into his office every day for a briefing. Gabriel, a veteran of several missions, finally told Fred that maybe he was overdoing the briefings.

At last, Gabriel departed for Nazareth (after one last briefing) and everyone held their breath.

Operation Christmas was underway.

Success!

Success

Gabriel was a pro.

Everyone watched his poise and perfect timing. The Annunciation scene, everyone agreed, would have made a perfect oil painting.

When Gabriel returned to heaven, there was a great celebration. Fred, not normally given to such things, passed out cigars.

Next came Mary's Visitation with Elizabeth, which went off like clockwork. There was a lesson here, Fred pointed out, for anyone who underestimated the value of careful planning.

Trouble

Things continued smoothly as the weeks went by.

Even Fred seemed to relax a bit.

Then it happened. The day began routinely enough with a general staff meeting, then everyone to their assigned tasks. Fred was in the Control Center when a very agitated staff member burst into his office.

"Sir, we've got trouble. Real trouble."

Fred breathed a barely audible sigh, then spoke without looking up. "Before you say another word, get hold of yourself. Whatever the problem, I'm sure it can be handled without raising your voice."

"Sir, Joseph and Mary are getting a divorce!"

"There now, see. I told you there was nothing…Getting a divorce? Have you lost your mind?"

"No, sir. It's the truth. Joseph found out that Mary was pregnant and now he's going to divorce her, and…"

"Joseph 'found out' that Mary was pregnant? Who, may I ask, was assigned to inform Joseph about this? If some staff member missed an assignment…"

"No one forgot, sir. It was all set for next week. Somehow Joseph found out earlier than we expected and now, well, that's it. He's filing for divorce."

Fred's administrative instincts regained control.

"Get Gabriel in here right away. We'll send him down there to straighten this mess out. A DIVORCE! What in the world…"

Gabriel met with Fred and then left quickly. He appeared to Joseph in a dream, quietly explained a few things, and that was that.

The divorce was off.

Actually, Joseph took the whole thing a lot better than Fred (who had to go to bed for a few days). Before doing so, Fred called an emergency staff meeting and pointed out that it would be better not to talk about this unfortunate glitch with anyone (including the front office).

Divorce talk, after all, could be very embarrassing for the Holy Family.

More Trouble

As the months passed, things went calmly along.

Fred grew a bit more tense, but that was understandable. Everyone was getting excited as the due date drew near.

Then, with the birth only days away, the impossible happened.

There was a soft knock at Fred's door, and a staff member stood before him looking very scared.

"Sir, ah, I don't think you're going to like this. I don't even like telling you. Actually, it caught all of us by surprise, and I'm sure you're going to be surprised too. Well, ah, to come right to the point…Joseph and Mary just packed their bags and left Nazareth. They're headed for Bethlehem."

"They did what? Now you look here! BETHLEHEM? I've got an angelic choir all choreographed for Nazareth. I've got three Magi on their way to Nazareth! I've got a star rising in the east and headed for Nazareth. I've got this scale model right here."

Fred pointed to the model, exact to the smallest detail. "DOES THAT LOOK LIKE BETHLEHEM?"

"You see, sir, Caesar Augustus issued this decree, and he said everyone had to…"

"CAESAR AUGUSTUS! Who's supposed to be handling foreign affairs?"

"We tried to get through, sir, but Caesar doesn't even believe in us, and he wouldn't listen, and…"

"Get the staff together right away, everybody! We're going to have to start rerouting everything, including that touchy choir. Get the charts! Get the maps! CAESAR AUGUSTUS! That miserable, heathen, infidel…"

Within hours Fred produced a totally revised plan (he called it "Plan B") and set everyone working round the clock. The hardest thing was moving the star without creating panic all over the world.

The second hardest thing was redoing the choreography for the choir.

Still More Trouble

A few days later, just when everything seemed back on course, a very nervous staff member once again stood before Fred.

"Ah, sir, I have sort of good news and bad news. First of all, I am happy to report that Mary and Joseph arrived safely in Bethlehem. By the way, it's a beautiful little town. Have you had a chance to see it?"

Fred glared at him and then pointed to his scale model. "Does this look like Bethlehem? IT'S NAZARETH…which, as you may recall, was where this whole thing was supposed to take place! I never even HEARD of Bethlehem until two days ago…and no, thank you, I HAVEN'T HAD TIME TO WALTZ DOWN THERE AND TAKE A PEEK AT IT!"

The angel hadn't even gotten to the bad news yet.

"Well, ah, anyway, it seems there was a slight snag. You see, this decree of Caesar Augustus has really jammed things up. Every room is booked for 10 miles. Well, anyway, Mary and Joseph got there a little faster than we expected and, ah, to come right to the point…they couldn't find a room. They're in sort of makeshift accommodations."

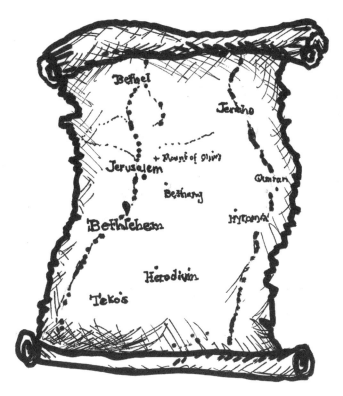

"MAKESHIFT ACCOMMODATIONS? YOU MEAN TO STAND THERE AND TELL ME THAT THE SON OF GOD…"

Fred's voice went dead. His face twisted as he struggled for control. Then he began to speak slowly.

"I've been working around the clock trying to move a star, to say nothing of redoing the choreography for that picky bunch of musicians, plus trying to get through to three Magi who are already on their way…I'm doing all that and not one of you geniuses even thought of GETTING A ROOM FOR THEM? Maybe you wizards think the Messiah, the King of Kings, should be born in a BARN or something!"

The angel shuffled nervously.

"Ah, well, you see, sir…You know, you're uncanny. I can see why they gave you this job. Actually, it's not quite a barn. More like a cave. Well, not exactly. It's a cave, but also a stable. You'd be surprised how clean it is, and…"

"A CAVE? A STABLE?…YOU HAVE GOT TO BE… You're not serious! Tell me you're not serious! Please tell me…"

Fred stared straight ahead, in a trance…his lips moving but making no sound. The angel saw his chance and left.

For a long time Fred stayed alone in his office. The staff huddled in small groups, spoke in whispers, and tiptoed whenever they had to pass by his office door.

As the Savior's birth approached, a hush came upon the entire Control Center. It was a beautiful event and many commented that the unexpected setting was even better than the one they had planned.

Still More Trouble

Fred finally emerged from his office. He looked exhausted. "Has the front office called?"

"No, sir. Everyone has been watching Christmas. It was beautiful. Too bad you missed it!"

Fred said nothing. You could tell he had been thinking.

"Maybe," he said, "maybe we can still salvage something. Any report on the angelic choir yet?"

"No, sir. They left on schedule a few minutes ago and we should be getting an update soon."

"Notify me as soon as we have any news."

News on the Choir

The news was not long in coming, and it was not good.

The staff drew straws to see who would tell Fred.

As fate would have it, the short straw fell to the same angel who brought Fred the news about the barn. He knocked gently on Fred's door, took a deep breath, and went in.

"Sir, we've received the latest bulletin on the angelic choir and, ah, to tell you the absolute truth, it's not exactly what we were hoping for. I'm sorry to have to keep bringing you this kind of news, sir, but perhaps in the long run these things aren't as bad as they seem. Why, I remember one time…"

"What about the BULLETIN?" Fred snapped.

"Well, sir, ah, the flight crew seems to have missed Bethlehem and ended up a little off-target. They didn't miss by much but, ah, to tell the absolute truth, it was a field. They didn't know what to do, but after a whole century of practice they decided to sing their song anyway. There were a couple of shepherds there, and some sheep. They all seemed to like it and…"

Fred slowly rose to his feet.

"You mean to stand there and tell me that after a whole century of rehearsals...after arranging and rearranging the choreography so that every prima donna could be seen... after all that fuss about their outfits...you mean to stand there and tell me that this heavenly, angelic choir went down there to a FIELD and sang to a couple of riff-raff SHEP-HERDS...and...and...SHEEP?"

"Well, sir, I can understand how you feel, but they said the flight plan was changed and…"

"I KNOW the flight plan was changed. This whole thing, as you may recall, was supposed to take place in Nazareth until those bungling fools in foreign relations let Caesar Augustus send Joseph and Mary packing to Bethlehem! Don't tell ME about changing the flight plan! I AM SICK AND TIRED OF HEARING…"

Fred sputtered and the angel tried to escape.

"COME BACK HERE!"

The angel turned around slowly. Fred had slumped into his chair.

After a few moments, Fred began to speak again.

"The visit of the Magi is our one last hope for ANY semblance of class. Maybe you geniuses could find some way of fouling up that one. Get out there and bring me the latest bulletin on the Magi!"

The angel left the office and found the staff huddled together reading the latest bulletin on the Magi.

Time to get out the straws again. There was a minor dis-agreement when the angel who had just returned from Fred's office announced that he would not, repeat, NOT be part of the drawing.

Another unfortunate courier was chosen.

He knocked lightly at Fred's door, hoping that perhaps he had fallen asleep from exhaustion.

"COME IN!" (So much for false hopes.)

"Sir, we received the bulletin on the Magi and, ah, it's not entirely good news. On the other hand, they say that God writes straight with crooked lines. I remember one time…"

"Just give me the bulletin! Maybe if you and your crack crew stopped writing sermonettes and started doing your work, we wouldn't be in this mess and the Messiah wouldn't be down there in a CAVE somewhere."

"Well, sir, as I was about to say, ah, well…the Magi are lost."

"The Magi are lost? LOST? You can't be serious. I put a star up there in the sky to show the way…A WHOLE STAR…and they turn around and get LOST?"

"Well, sir, they said you moved the star and…"

"I KNOW I moved the star. This whole thing, as you may recall, was supposed to take place in Nazareth until those bumbling, bungling, babbling…"

Fred became incoherent.

Unfortunately, the angel wasn't finished with the bad news. "Ah, there is something else. You see, well…let me put it this way. You'll never guess who they asked for directions."

Fred started to laugh, not the kind of laughter you wanted to hear.

"Guess who they asked for directions? GUESS WHO THEY ASKED FOR DIRECTIONS? Sure! I'll play your silly game. The way you experts handled things they probably asked the one person in the whole world who was absolutely forbidden to know anything about this. Go ahead and tell me. GO AHEAD AND TELL ME. TELL ME THEY ASKED 'CRAZY HEROD!'"

"Wow. I can see why they gave you this job. You hit it right on the button. It was 'crazy Herod.' You see, when they lost track of the star, they…"

Fred never heard the rest of the story. He had fainted.

The staff gathered to watch the arrival of the Magi. Nobody seemed to mind that they were a little late. And the gifts were well received.

The scene closed like the ending of a movie with everyone disappearing slowly over the horizon...the Magi going back to the mysterious East, and the Holy Family traveling south to Egypt.

The angels watched silently, then went to clean out their desks.

Operation Christmas was over.

40

* * *

When our best plans go awry,
it might help to remember that sometimes God does indeed
write straight with crooked lines.

MERRY CHRISTMAS!

Ken Untener was the Bishop of the Catholic Diocese of Saginaw, Michigan. He was a native Detroiter, who attended Sacred Heart Seminary in Detroit, and St. John's Provincial Seminary in Plymouth, Michigan. In 1963, he was ordained by Cardinal John F. Dearden as a priest for the Archdiocese of Detroit.

After parish work and then service in the Chancery, he was sent to the Pontifical Gregorian University in Rome where he obtained his doctorate in dogmatic theology. He returned to Detroit and served in the Clergy Office.

In 1977 he was appointed Rector of St. John's Provincial Seminary. In November of 1980, he became the fourth bishop of the Diocese of Saginaw, where he served until his death in 2004.

His articles appeared in various periodicals, and he wrote two books, "Sunday Liturgy Can Be Better," and "Preaching Better." He regularly gave retreats to priests and theological/pastoral talks around the country.